LET'S GET A RIDE

TJ Cat and the Superheroes

Israelin Shockness

VANQUEST PUBLISHING
motivating | inspiring | educating

SERIES: TJ CAT AND THE SUPERHEROES
BOOK 2

Cataloguing in Publication Data
Author – Israelin Shockness, PhD

ISBN: 978-1-989480-07-6 (ebook)
ISBN: 978-1-989480-06-9 (paperback)

Series: TJ Cat and the Superheroes | Book 2

DEDICATION
TO MY FAMILY

It was the second day of school for TJ Cat.

"Wake up, Sleepy Head," his mom called out from the kitchen. But TJ Cat was already up. He had brushed his teeth and had gotten dressed for school.

When TJ Cat rushed downstairs, his mom was surprised to see him down so soon. She had packed his lunch and snacks in his Superman lunchbox.

She was just about to fix his favorite breakfast, scrambled eggs and hashed browns, when TJ Cat asked, "May I have cereal, please?"

"Sure." TJ Cat's mom was puzzled, but she poured a little cereal and some milk into his bowl.

After eating his cereal, TJ Cat picked up his lunchbox, said goodbye, and was about to leave for school.

"But aren't you waiting for me?" his mom asked.

"No, you don't have to come. I can go by myself."

After a minute or so, his mom said, "Go straight to the bus stop. No playing on the way!"

But before TJ Cat could answer, his mom added,
"Make sure you walk on the sidewalk. And look both ways before you cross the street."

"Yes, Mom, I know that," TJ Cat answered proudly.

TJ Cat was happy that his mom was not going to walk with him to the bus stop.

At the bus stop, TJ Cat met his new friends, Puppy D and BoxerPup. They gave each other a high five.

BoxerPup, who was facing the road, shouted, "Look, there's a new little animal coming to our bus stop."

As the other two little animals turned around quickly to look, they saw that the school bus had just arrived. Puppy D, TJ Cat and BoxerPup rushed on to the bus to get seats close together.

From his seat beside her, Puppy D looked across at the new little animal. She smiled at him. He smiled back and asked what her name was.

"I'm Maisy, Maisy Monkey."

"I am Puppy D. These are my two friends. This is TJ Cat and this is BoxerPup."

TJ Cat and BoxerPup smiled. The four little animals began to chat. They were becoming friends.

Then Puppy D, TJ Cat, and BoxerPup talked about school and about the superhero club.

"What is the superhero club?" Maisy Monkey asked. They told her about the club and about their superheroes.

"That's great," said Maisy Monkey. "I have a superhero, too. My superhero is my mom. She likes Sunrise Animal School, because she says it's very friendly".

Still sitting on the bus, the little friends were all looking through the window. The traffic was very heavy and the bus was almost stopped.

"Look, there are two little animals walking to school, one behind the other," said Puppy D.

"They look tired," noted TJ Cat.

"They will be late for school," Barry BrownBear observed.

After a few minutes, the traffic cleared and the bus was again on its way to school.

The little animals decided to play a game of counting the number of red cars they could see before reaching school.

When TJ Cat and his friends arrived at school, Miss Cheval was already in the classroom. She welcomed her new student, Maisy Monkey, and gave her a new workbook.

Then TJ Cat asked Miss Cheval, "When will we talk about the superhero club?"

"Sometime after lunch," Miss Cheval noted.

TJ Cat and the other little animals took out their pens and pencils and started working in the workbooks that Miss Cheval had placed on their desks earlier.

"Good show," Miss Cheval encouraged the little animals, as she walked around and saw them all writing in their workbooks.

Just before morning recess, the two little animals that were walking to school finally arrived.

"They just got here!" Puppy D blurted out, as he and his friends dashed out to the playground.

Miss Cheval spoke to the two new animals that had just arrived at school, while the other little animals were playing outside.

After recess, Miss Cheval introduced the two new little animals to the class. "This is Baba Bear and his twin sister, Bonny Bear. They lost their ride on their way to school this morning."

"What happened?" Freddy Frog asked.

Baba Bear explained that their dad's car broke down on their way to school.

Paula Piggy asked, "Will your car be fixed by tomorrow?"

"I don't think so. The last time it broke down, it took a few days to get fixed." Bonny Bear sounded sad.

"So you can't come to school tomorrow?" asked Freddy Frog.

"We don't know yet," said Baba Bear.

"But if you need a ride, then maybe someone can give you a ride?" Paula Piggy noted.

"I can give you a ride on my back," Ellie Elephant said, "but we'll all be late for school."

All the little animals giggled.

Then Miss Cheval said to the class, "Well, let's do some reading now." She began reading a short story from a book she got in the library.

The little animals really enjoyed stories, so they sat quietly while Miss Cheval read.

It was soon lunch time. TJ Cat and some of the other little animals sat in a circle on the carpet in the room next to their classroom.

Baba Bear and Bonny Bear sat on the carpet with TJ Cat, BoxerPup, Puppy D and Matt Monkey, and they talked and laughed as they ate their lunches.

"Where do you live," asked Matt Monkey. The other little animals found out that the Bears lived very far from the school.

Baba Bear explained: "Dad wanted us to go to the Bear Academy near us to learn how to run and play with other bears our own age."

"But Mom really wanted us to come to the Sunrise Animal School where we could meet and make friends with different little animals besides just bears," Bonny Bear added. "And Dad finally agreed."

CLASSROOM RULES:

Little Animals,
Please keep this space clean.

No eating beyond this point.

Right after lunch, Miss Cheval said to the class, "Now we can talk about the superhero club.

Baba Bear and Bonny Bear were curious and asked many questions about the club. Puppy D noted that the club was just starting off.

"Do you like our club?" Freddy Frog asked.

"Sure," the twins answered at the same time as if they were one little animal. The other little animals giggled.

After a while, Maisy Monkey suggested, "Maybe the superhero club could help them get a ride to school."

"That's a good idea," Miss Cheval added. "How would you go about this?"

After many ideas, the little animals decided to write notes from the superhero club to their parents asking for help. Miss Cheval agreed that it could work.

Miss Cheval helped the little animals to make up the notes for their parents, and allowed the little animals to use her phone number on the notes. She also made sure she had the twins' phone number.

The little animals spent the whole afternoon printing the notes to take home. TJ Cat prayed that someone would offer to give the twin bears a ride to school.

All evening TJ Cat talked about the notes with his mom, and wished that Baba Bear and Bonny Bear would get a ride to school. He really liked them.

The next morning, TJ Cat saw that his wish had come true. The twin bears were at school. A farmer, Mr. Collie, had seen a note and offered to take the bears to school when he would go to the market in the mornings.

Bonny Bear was happy. "Dad said the superhero club did a good thing for us. Thanks, Superhero Club. Thanks Miss Cheval. Thanks everyone."

Miss Cheval nodded her head and said to the little animals, "Your superhero club is really doing good things. Keep it up."

Puppy D, who was not sure the notes would work so quickly, said, "Our Animal Superhero Club has done its first good thing. We now have to find other good things to do. This is what superheroes do!"

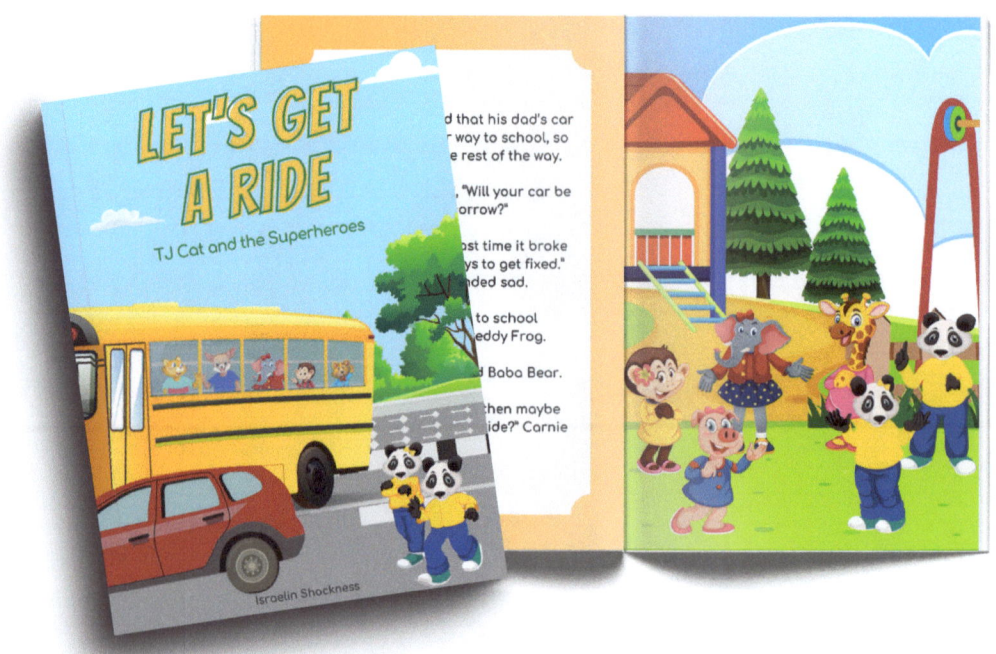

HOPE YOU ENJOY OUR BOOKS.

You just read Book 2 of the series, TJ Cat and the Superheroes. Please leave a review at Amazon or where you bought this book.

SEE THE OTHER BOOKS COMING SOON TO THIS SERIES:

Book 3: A Surprise Gift: TJ Cat and the Superheroes
Book 4: Helping and Having Fun: TJ Cat and the Superheroes

ABOUT THE AUTHOR

Israelin Shockness, PhD, has been an educator for over 25 years, working with young children, youth and adult students. An author of a number of book series, she continues to write for and about children and youth. Israelin is also the author of several book-length biographies, and writes and consults on writing in this genre. She can be reached at info@IsraelinShockness.com

www.ingramcontent.com/pod-product-compliance
Lightning Source LLC
Chambersburg PA
CBHW041013170626
46815CB00003B/281